# T.G. and MOONIE
## Go Shopping

Story by Fay Maschler

## Pictures by
## SYLVIE SELIG
Doubleday & Company, Inc.

Garden City, New York

*Also by Sylvie Selig and Fay Maschler*

T.G. AND MOONIE MOVE OUT OF TOWN

ISBN: 0-385-14147-5 Trade
      0-385-14148-3 Prebound

Library of Congress Catalog Card Number 77-18451

Text Copyright © 1978 by Fay Maschler
Illustrations Copyright © 1978 by Sylvie Selig

First Edition in the United States of America

Printed in Great Britain

T.G. and Moonie were going
shopping. The house needed some
things. "Hurry up, Moonie,"
demanded T.G. "The angle
of my hat is not right yet," she said.

They set off for the village,
but Moonie stopped
to look at the flowers.
Moonie seems to dawdle a lot,
thought T.G., but he
held his tongue.
They planned to buy a present for
Bernard – the owl they live with.

"It's been quite a long time
since *I've* had a present,"
muttered Blott, their pet.

On the way, they met the dog
who loves to go fishing.
"My boys have brought their rod
and net," he said. "Maybe we'll
be able to bring you
some nice fish
for your supper."

I'll buy some food anyway,
just in case,
thought Moonie.

In the village they were not
quite sure where to begin.
"Should have made a
list, Moonie." "Yes," she said.
Blott stopped on High Street
outside a pet shop.

"First things first," said T.G.
(as he often did), and they
went to the hardware shop
to buy a basket.
"Can you show me that one
at the very top?" Moonie asked.
They looked around for Blott,
but he was nowhere.
"Maybe we'll see him on
the way to the grocer's, dear,"
said T.G.

"There's not a single orange
in the house," said Moonie,
and she loaded the basket.
"A dozen will be plenty," said T.G.,
squeezing one for juiciness.

Outside, sticking out of a box
belonging to a team of
performing birds, was something
that looked very much
like Blott's tail.

"Oh, my quivering whiskers," shrieked Moonie, "that thing we thought was Blott is a little stripy snake." "Calm yourself, Moonie," said T.G., and he kept looking at the muscles of the big strong bird. The couple from the hardware shop suggested that Blott might have gone to look at the toys. "He could be choosing himself a present, you know."

There were toys and games
that looked like Blott's tail,
but none turned out
to be Blott.
Moonie was very sad.
The shopkeeper suggested
that Blott might be looking
at the antique market
in the street.
"There are lots of things there
that might interest a young pet,"
she said.

At the antique market
they saw an old
wooden spoon handle
that just for a moment
looked like Blott's tail.
But no Blott was attached.
"We've got a radio and
Bernard's got a wind-up
record player, but that
old blue bike would make
him a perfect present.
He could use it on his
nighttime rounds," said
Moonie. And I could borrow it
during the day, thought T.G.
"What a good idea, my love,"
he said. "Let's buy it."

"I think I'll just call Bernard
on the phone," said Moonie.
"Blott may have gone home
on his own." "Don't tell Bernard
about the bike," hissed T.G.
Just at that moment Blott
trotted up with a gold
antique fob-watch
in his mouth.

T.G. and Moonie were so pleased that they invited all their new friends – the couple from the hardware shop, the kind lady who sells toys, the sympathetic pigs and the performing birds – to the tea shop for some creamy cakes. Moonie cuddled Blott, who held on tightly to the gold fob-watch.

They set off for home.
"Come and see us in our
new house," they shouted
to their new friends.

But telephone first,
thought Moonie.

Bicycling back, Moonie on the crossbar, they met the dog who loves fishing, with his sons. They have had some luck today. I hope they will bring us some fish, thought Moonie. Oranges never made a meal.

At home Bernard was waiting for them at the window. T.G. and Moonie had a little kiss after their tiring day.

Bernard was overjoyed with his present. "Now I'll be able to explore much further," he said. And I don't know another owl with a blue two-wheeler bike, he thought to himself.
Blott, who hadn't said a word, handed Bernard the gold antique fob-watch.
Oh Blott, thought Moonie, how nice. I thought you had bought it for yourself.

"Be back at dawn, I mean,
5:30 a.m.," Bernard said,
looking at his watch and
ringing his bicycle bell.

Friends to come home
to, he thought.
What could be better?

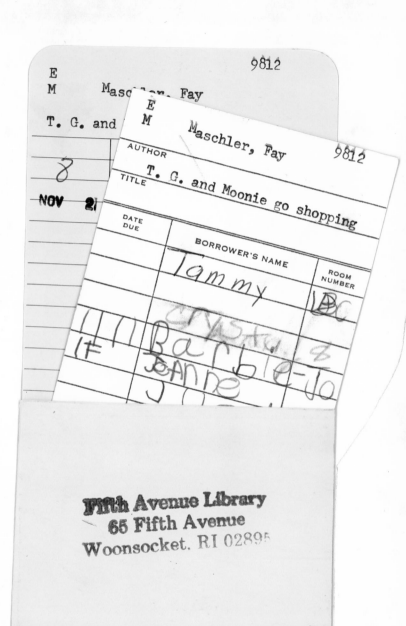

E
M
Mas~~chler,~~ Fay                    9812

T. G. and

8

**NOV** 2

IF

E
M
Maschler, Fay                    9812

AUTHOR

T. G. and Moonie go shopping

TITLE

| DATE DUE | BORROWER'S NAME | ROOM NUMBER |
|---|---|---|
| | Tammy | |
| | Crystal | 8 |
| | Barbie-Jo | |
| | JeAnne | |